DEATH WHEELS

Presented to you by
Alsager School

Titles in Teen Reads:

Fascination
DANIEL BLYTHE

I Spy
DANIEL BLYTHE

New Dawn
DANIEL BLYTHE

Underworld
SIMON CHESHIRE

Dawn of the Daves
TIM COLLINS

Joke Shop
TIM COLLINS

Mr Perfect
TIM COLLINS

Painkiller
TIM COLLINS

The Locals
TIM COLLINS

Troll
TIM COLLINS

Wasteland
TIM COLLINS

Copy Cat
TOMMY DONBAVAND

Dead Scared
TOMMY DONBAVAND

Just Bite
TOMMY DONBAVAND

Home
TOMMY DONBAVAND

Kidnap
TOMMY DONBAVAND

Raven
TOMMY DONBAVAND

Ward 13
TOMMY DONBAVAND

Fair Game
ALAN DURANT

Blank
ANN EVANS

By My Side
ANN EVANS

Living the Lie
ANN EVANS

Nightmare
ANN EVANS

Insectoids
ROGER HURN

Vanishing Point
CHERYL LANYON

Jigsaw Lady
TONY LEE

Mister Scratch
TONY LEE

Noticed
TONY LEE

Stalker
TONY LEE

Death Road
JON MAYHEW

Death Wheels
JON MAYHEW

The First Martian
IAIN MC LAUGHLIN

Snow White,
Black Heart
JACQUELINE RAYNER

Silent Nation
BEVERLY SANFORD

Remember Rosie
BEVERLY SANFORD

The Wishing Doll
BEVERLY SANFORD

Billy Button
CAVAN SCOTT

Mama Barkfingers
CAVAN SCOTT

Pest Control
CAVAN SCOTT

The Changeling
CAVAN SCOTT

The Hunted
CAVAN SCOTT

Sitting Target
JOHN TOWNSEND

Deadly Mission
MARK WRIGHT

Ghost Bell
MARK WRIGHT

The Corridor
MARK WRIGHT

World Without Words
JONNY ZUCKER

Badger Publishing Limited, Oldmedow Road, Hardwick Industrial Estate, King's Lynn PE30 4JJ
Telephone: 01438 791037

www.badgerlearning.co.uk

DEATH WHEELS

JON MAYHEW

Death Wheels ISBN 978-1-78464-619-6

Publisher: Susan Ross
Senior Editor: Danny Pearson
Editorial Coordinator: Claire Morgan
Copyeditor: Cambridge Publishing Management
Designer: Bigtop Design Ltd
Cover: © YAY Media AS / Alamy Stock Photo

2 4 6 8 10 9 7 5 3 1

In the year 2320 the Great Disaster happened.

A nuclear war destroyed all the main towns and cities of the world.

The water dried up and the world became one big desert.

Then a plague came. It turned ordinary people into flesh-hungry zombies.

The unaffected survivors built walls around what was left of their cities to keep out the zombies.

But there were worse things than zombies. And they were watching.

This is the world Omak lives in.

CHAPTER 1

Omak saw the smoke drifting up from the horizon. The desert stretched out around him in all directions but the smoke was right in his path.

It could mean trouble, he thought, as he drove his dune buggy towards it. *Or maybe something interesting!*

Omak's small red car bounced over rocks and dried-out tree trunks, its thick knobbly wheels biting into the rough sandy ground. Omak called the car the Blood Bug. He was a Postie and he used it to travel between cities, delivering messages and parcels for the people of Birmingham. Petrol was in short supply in this barren dried-up world and so some Posties powered their armour-plated cars with cooking oil, or solar power or a bit of both. They travelled light to save fuel and so the smallest were often the most successful. That's why most Posties were kids of fifteen or sixteen.

As Omak drew nearer, he saw a man standing on the roof of a burning car. Smoke billowed out of the car's bonnet. At any minute the whole thing could blow up. But Omak could understand why the man wasn't jumping down in a hurry. Snappers pressed themselves against the body of the car and grabbed for the man.

Once, the snappers had been human just like Omak, but after the Great Disaster they got a disease and changed into ravenous zombies. They never slept. They just wandered in the hot waterless land that surrounded the walled city of Birmingham, mindless and hungry. Omak could see their yellow teeth and their grey skin. They reached out with long black fingernails. To them, the old man was just meat.

The thick smoke made it hard for Omak to see the man clearly but when the man fell off the car, Omak gasped. He had to do something.

There were eight snappers, Omak reckoned. He slammed his foot onto the accelerator and aimed the Blood Bug straight at them. Three bounced over the front of his car with a crunch and a thud. He whirled the steering wheel, stopping alongside the burning car.

Two snappers stood right in front of him, staring and trying to figure out what to do next. They weren't smart. What was left of their dried-out brains could only think of food. They moved slowly. The danger was getting trapped by a pack of them like this man had. Revving the engine, Omak sent the Blood Bug hurtling forward. The snappers didn't even try to get out of the way and they disappeared under the front wheels.

Three left, Omak thought. He grabbed the baseball bat that rested at the side of his seat and jumped out. The three remaining snappers crouched over the old man. Omak just hoped he wasn't too late. With a yell, he leaped forward, whirling the bat. The snappers turned round, half standing to see what the new source of food was. Omak's bat smacked sideways across the head of the first snapper. This one was old, dried out by years in the hot sun. Its neck looked like an old dead branch and it was just as brittle. The snapper's head went sailing into the burning car and its body crumpled to the ground.

"Two left!" Omak shouted, swinging the baseball bat again. Another snapper fell. "One!" But even one snapper could be dangerous. If it bit you, broke your skin even a tiny bit, then the snapper virus would infect you and change you into one of them. Omak crouched, watching the last snapper. It seemed confused. It didn't know who to go for. As it stood, looking from the man to Omak and back, Omak struck, swinging the bat hard. It struck the snapper's skull with a loud crack and the creature fell to the ground like a puppet that had had its strings cut.

For a moment, Omak stood panting for breath, just looking at the twisted bodies that lay on the ground. Then the man groaned. Omak leaped forward to help him.

He was old with long grey hair and beard. His leather jacket was cracked by the heat of the sun and his clothes were ragged. Blood streamed from a horrible wound on his neck and his face was scorched black and red from the car fire. He gasped for breath and grabbed Omak's hand.

"When I die," he groaned. "Burn my body. Please. You can have anything from my pockets. I haven't got much…" he coughed and blood trickled from his mouth. "Just don't let me… change!" he nodded at the dead snappers.

"I understand, old man," Omak said. "I'll make sure you're safe."

"Here," said the old man, handing Omak a scrappy piece of paper in his trembling hands. "Take this..."

Omak frowned and unfolded the paper. "It's a map," he said, studying the lines and symbols. Omak had been to school long enough to read and do sums but after that it was the school of life and the university of driving through snappers. He could see his city, Birmingham, and he recognised some of the other names on it. One word wasn't familiar to him. "What's this?" he spelled it out. "R-e-f-i-n-e-r-y..."

"That's a refinery, sonny. Oil, petrol," the old man said, his eyes shone. "Lakes of it underground. Just there for the taking!"

Omak's eyes widened. "A refinery! Where they used to make fuel for cars and lorries?" he gasped. He'd learned about it in History. People had taken things like petrol and water for granted. Omak could never believe it.

"Nobody knows it's there," the old man said, his breath becoming heavier. "Only me. Whoever finds it can take it. Looks like it's you..."

"Imagine," Omak whispered. "Enough fuel to power the city. I'll be rich. Mum'll be so proud!"

The old man's face clouded over and he gritted his teeth. "You gotta be careful, though," he gasped. "Watch out for... trogs..."

Omak frowned. "Watch out for what?"

But the old man lay still.

Omak sighed. The old man's car blazed now. It was only a matter of time before the old man became a snapper. Omak heaved the body onto his shoulder and threw it onto the burning car as the old man had asked. Then Omak climbed into the Blood Bug, the map on the seat next to him. He grinned. He couldn't wait to tell his mum. Maybe his luck had changed. In his excitement, he forgot the old man's troubled face and his dying words of warning.

CHAPTER 2

As soon as Omak had driven in through the huge gates of Birmingham and parked the Blood Bug safely, he hurried down the dusty narrow back streets to his house. The mudbrick buildings were held up with parts of old buildings and made the city look like a huge rubbish dump but it was home to him.

Omak hurried up the stairs to his flat and pushed the door open. He couldn't wait to tell Mum about the map that was going to change their lives. Mum and her new partner, Fergal, stood by the scrubbed table, getting some food ready.

"Mum! Guess what happened today…"

But Mum raised a hand. She looked excited too; had she found out about the map and the refinery already? How? "Omak wait," she said. "We've got some exciting news. Fergal has got something to say."

Fergal looked surprised. He was a big man with a thick red beard and broad shoulders. He was tough and could look after himself but next to Mum, he looked like a startled rabbit about to be run over. "I have?" he said, glancing at her. "Oh! Yes!" He cleared his throat. "Thing is, Omak, I need an apprentice to help me work on the water works. It'd be a regular job, with weekly pay and a food allowance from the Governing Council. You'd be learning a trade, digging and clearing waterways."

Mum's eyes shone with excitement. "It'd be safe, Omak," she said. "I'd know where you were. I wouldn't have to worry any more about whether or not you'd broken down somewhere out in the desert between here and London. We'd have more money coming in and you wouldn't be searching around for work all the time, never sure when the next job was going to come up or how dangerous it would be. What do you think?"

Omak's shoulders drooped. "Oh."

"Well aren't you pleased?" Mum said.

"Um, yeah," Omak said. He looked up at Fergal. "Thanks. Can I think about it?"

Fergal shrugged. "Sure you can," he said. "I thought you'd have jumped at the chance. You're always grumbling about driving out into the desert and telling us how dangerous it is."

"It's just," Omak began to say but he caught a glimpse of Mum's worried face. Before Fergal had come along, life had been tough. Every penny Omak and Mum had earned was spent by the end of the week. They had been constantly searching for ways to make ends meet. Omak knew that if they didn't pay the rent, they'd be thrown out of the tiny flat and if they didn't pay off their food and water debts, then they'd have to work as slaves down in the sewers.

Since Fergal had moved in, life had got easier. Omak had even been able to upgrade the Blood Bug to a two-seater. He sighed. "It's just that... well, the water works are a bit... boring..." He felt bad the moment he said it. He liked Fergal.

"If by 'boring' you mean not nearly getting eaten by snappers every day or not crashing your car or not getting robbed by bandits, then yes, it probably is boring. But life would get a lot more interesting if Fergal wasn't fixing the water supply for this city. Imagine that!"

Omak groaned. His mum was like a terrier when she started on at him. Her dark eyes glittered with fury. And it was true. Some days, he hated getting into his car. Some days, he felt frightened by what he saw outside the city walls. He didn't like the idea of Mum worrying too.

"OK! OK!" he said at last. "I'll think about it. Just get off my back!" Omak stormed out of the flat and back down the stairs. *I'll find Silva, see what she thinks*, he thought.

***

Silva Dacosta was in her workshop with her head buried in the engine of her car, Blue Flash.

"Why would you want to work on the water works?" she said, the engine cavity making her voice sound hollow. "Sounds dull."

"It's safer and better money, I guess," he replied. He never understood why Silva was a Postie. Her family were quite rich and she had gone to school until she was a teenager. She could have the pick of the jobs available in Birmingham. "Anyway, I haven't decided yet. I wanted to show you something." Omak pulled out the map.

Silva's eyes lit up as Omak told her about the old man and his story about the lost oil refinery.

"Omak, we've got to go!" she said. "It's too good to miss!"

"That's what I thought," Omak muttered, folding the map up. "But it's too dangerous. How do we know it's true? The old man was pretty chewed up. And what if the map's wrong. It's pretty rough."

Silva frowned. "You don't want to go and look for it?" She said. "I thought you'd jump at the chance!"

"I don't know what I want to do," Omak snapped.

"Well, you're a fool if you miss this opportunity," Silva said. "What are you going to do? Fix water pipes instead?"

"It's all right for you," Omak said. "My mum says..."

Silva let out a huge laugh. "Your mum?" She said. "What's up? Won't Mummy let you go?

Well, I tell you what, Omak, if you don't want to go and find that refinery, I will."

Omak ground his teeth. Then he threw the map at her. "Be my guest. I hope you find a nest of snappers instead of a refinery!" Omak strode out of the workshop. "I've had enough of adventure. I'm going to make some real money instead of scrambling across the dirt for pennies."

"You'll come running after me!" Silva shouted and Omak heard the clink of a spanner hitting the ground.

"No chance!" Omak muttered. He was leaving his driving life behind him forever. Or so he thought.

CHAPTER 3

The water works were quite far from Omak's flat. A huge pump drew water from deep under the earth. The water was stored in massive water tanks that covered the area and rose up above the walls that kept the city safe. The plant filled the eastern part of the city where some of the wealthier families lived in big houses, close to the water. Some even had small gardens. Omak had never seen anything like it.

"Work hard, Omak, and you might be living in a house like that one day," Fergal had said.

Several weeks had passed since Omak started working with Fergal at the water works. Now he sat on top of one of the water tanks looking out across the desert. Clouds of dust swirled in the distance, possibly a swarm of snappers or a Postie on a mission. Fergal clambered up the ladder and sat next to him.

"You wishing you were back out there?" Fergal said.

Omak shrugged. "Sort of," he said. "I haven't made the best start here, have I?"

"Nonsense!" Fergal said. "You know your way round the pumps like a professional!"

"That's because of all the time I've spent on the Blood Bug's engine," Omak said. "Anyway, I don't mean that."

"So you've had a few arguments with the workmen here..." Fergal began.

"A few?" Omak said. "I have one every day. I'm not used to being told what to do." He gave a smile. "Except by Mum, of course."

Fergal waggled his bushy red eyebrows. "Everyone does what *she* says, Omak." They both laughed.

Omak's smile soon faded. "I'm worried about Silva," he said. "She's been out there for too long."

Silva had taken Omak on his word and set off with the map and Turgen Emblek, another Postie. Omak had seen them drive off at first light about a week ago but had hidden in the shadows of the Western Gateway. He hadn't forgiven Silva for her taunt about being a mummy's boy. Besides, seeing her talking and laughing with Turgen made his stomach flip. He wanted to step out and punch Turgen in the nose, not that it would be a good idea. Turgen was about six feet tall and built like one of the water tanks.

"You really like her, don't you?" Fergal grinned.

Omak could feel his face going red. "She's a good friend," he said, not catching Fergal's eye. "But she hasn't come back and I feel responsible." Omak explained all about the old man and the map and Fergal let out a long slow whistle.

"With that much oil, the city could run for years. We could drill deeper for water," he said. "People's lives would be so much better."

Omak felt his cheeks going even redder. "I was just thinking how rich we'd be..."

Before Fergal could say anything, someone called Omak's name. He and Fergal hurried down the metal ladders that spiralled round the sides of the tanks. At the bottom of the ladder stood a policeman, looking stern and serious. Omak swallowed hard. What had he done?

"Mayor Lewis needs Omak at the council chambers right away," the policeman said. "It's about Silva Dacosta."

***

Mayor Lewis sat in the Council Chamber, where all the big decisions about the city were made. Omak had been here once before when he'd actually saved Mayor Lewis's life and the lives of the whole of the city of London too. The last mayor had tried to infect the city of London with Snapper virus and he took Lewis hostage. Omak and Silva had stopped him. "Omak," Mayor Lewis said, smiling. "Good to see you again."

Omak nodded. "Mayor Lewis," he said, feeling embarrassed. They weren't alone. A group of about ten people sat on either side of the Mayor and there was another person: young girl, pale and dressed in strange ragged clothes. "The officer said that there was news of Silva Dacosta," Omak said. "Is she OK?"

"She's alive," Mayor Lewis said, looking down from his chair at the young girl. "This is Rosa. She came here with a strange tale. My dear, would you care to tell Omak what you told me?"

The girl swallowed and looked at Omak with huge pale eyes. With her wide mouth and staring eyes, she reminded Omak of a toad or a lizard. The moment he thought it, he felt guilty.

"I come from the refinery your friend Silva was looking for," the girl said. "She rescued me from some snappers and we ran into some caves there. It was dark and we were hiding from the snappers. Suddenly, Silva screamed and vanished from my side. She had fallen down a deep shaft in the caves. She was alive but hurt and told me to go and get help."

"How did you find your way here?" Omak said.

Rosa fumbled in her pocket and pulled out the map. Omak took it. It was more crumpled, now, smudged with dust and what looked like dried blood. "Silva threw this up to me."

"And you travelled all on your own?" Omak said in amazement. The girl was small. He couldn't really figure out her age. She looked like a desert breeze would blow her over.

"I managed to meet up with a convoy of merchant trucks," she said. "Then a Postie picked me up." She glanced over at Mayor Lewis and smiled briefly. Omak shivered. Her teeth were small and pointed. "The Mayor paid him for my journey," she said.

"There was a boy with Silva," Omak said, he'd almost forgotten about Turgen. "What happened to him?"

Rosa shrugged and slipped a strand of lank hair behind her large ear. "I didn't see a boy and she never mentioned one. She just told me to get help."

The Mayor stood up. "Normally, I wouldn't get involved," he said. "What happens to people who choose to venture outside these walls is their business, as you know, Omak. But you and Silva once did this city a great service and I find I can't leave Silva to her fate."

Omak nodded. It was true that Silva was just as responsible for saving the Mayor, and plenty more people besides, many months ago. "I can go and find her," Omak said.

The Mayor smiled. "I was hoping you would say that," he said. "Sadly, I can't send anyone with you. The city guards are stretched to the limit with patrolling to keep snappers away. Every day sees more swarms of them at our walls, drawn by the people living inside. But I can offer you fuel, a complete overhaul for your buggy and provisions for the journey. Rosa will show you where Silva is."

"I'll do it," Omak said. "How soon can the engineers have the Blood Bug ready?"

The Mayor grinned again. "Forgive me but I thought you'd agree," he chuckled. "Your precious machine is being serviced now. You can leave at first light."

"Bring it on," Omak said, grinning.

CHAPTER 4

As Omak expected, Mum wasn't too pleased about his rescue mission. "It's too dangerous," she snapped, slamming Omak's dinner in front of him. "The fact that this Silva girl is in so much trouble shows that."

"But she's my friend, Mum," Omak said, quietly. "It's a mission for the Mayor too. He's said he'll pay me well for my time."

"If the Mayor's so keen to rescue Silva Dacosta, then why doesn't *he* go or send some soldiers?" she said, putting her hands on her hips.

"Nobody can be spared," Fergal cut in. "If he could, the Mayor would send some men but time is running out for the poor girl and Omak is fast."

Mum looked into Omak's eyes and hugged him close. "Well, you're going to go whatever I say, so be careful. Please come back safely."

Omak grinned. "Don't worry. I will," he said.

***

Quite a crowd had gathered to see Omak and Rosa off by the huge Western gate. The Blood Bug gleamed in the first rays of the sun. It looked brand new. Even the tiniest scuffs from the last time Omak had taken it out were polished away. He helped Rosa climb in and then jumped into the driving seat. New seats and a shiny new steering wheel. Omak grinned. The Mayor appeared alongside him, looking down. "I trust everything is in order, Omak," he said.

"Awesome!" Omak said, grinning even more.

The Mayor smiled briefly, then his face became serious. "You have the Dacosta family to thank for most of the upgrades. They want their daughter back. We all do," he said. "Good luck, Omak. Don't take any more chances than you have to but if you can, bring Silva back safely."

Omak nodded and then turned the ignition. The Blood Bug roared into life, startling even Omak. It sounded more powerful than ever. The gates opened and Omak looked over to Rosa who held the crumpled map in her white fists.

"You ready?" he said.

She nodded. Omak slammed his foot down on the accelerator and smiled as they powered forwards out of the walled city of Birmingham, out of safety, and straight towards danger.

***

The noise of the engine made it impossible for Omak to speak to Rosa. She sat in silence, her eyes gleaming. Every now and then, she would point to a track they should take or stare down at the map. Omak felt guilty but everything about her made his skin prickle. It wasn't that she just looked a bit creepy. He didn't like the way she stared at him while he was driving. Omak hated the way he looked. His front teeth were too big and his hair sprung out in all directions like an old, used brush. Of course, most of the time, he had to concentrate on the rocky, bumpy tracks they were following but he'd glance sidelong at her and catch her. He felt like she was laughing at him.

"You OK?" he yelled.

She nodded.

Omak didn't really travel west very often. His main journeys had taken him south or east, to London or Cambridge. Once or twice, he had headed north to Manchester but there wasn't much out to the west.

As the darkness grew, Rosa directed Omak to a cave in some rocks. Omak pulled a face. "I'm not sure," he muttered. "Is it safe?"

"I stayed there on the way to your city," she said. "You could park the car across the entrance to stop anything getting in."

Omak shrugged and they drove to the cave. It wasn't deep and when Omak shone his headlights into it, he could see it was empty. He drew the car up to block the cave mouth and then unpacked some of the food they had been given for the journey.

"We should keep our breathing masks on if we're going to sleep outside the main cabin of the buggy," Omak said. "The air doesn't seem too bad here but I wouldn't want to spend long exposed to it." He went gathering scraps of dead wood that littered the desert then lit a fire.

Soon they were chewing on bean stew and staring into the flames. Rosa didn't seem too hungry. "Do you have family at this refinery?" Omak asked her.

Rosa shook her head. "I did have but they died. Snappers got some of them but others just got sick and died," she said.

"You don't sound very sad about it," Omak muttered, fixing her with a suspicious gaze.

Rosa shrugged. "I was," she said simply. "But you have to survive, don't you? Trying to stay alive doesn't leave much time for sadness."

Omak nodded. "That's true," he said. "What's this refinery like, then?"

"It doesn't look much from the surface," she said, her eyes gleaming in the firelight. "The sand has covered it up. But when you go down into the maze of tunnels, there are rooms filled with strange coloured pipes and metal walls. There are huge halls filled with lakes of oil. It's amazing."

Omak grunted. “Funny that nobody has claimed it for their own,” he said, picking some bean stew from between his teeth.

“Some say that a dark and nameless evil dwells deep down in the lakes of oil,” Rosa whispered into the fire. “Besides, the land around it is poisoned. Nothing grows. Nothing can live there.”

“Except you and your family,” Omak reminded her.

A brief flash of anger crossed Rosa’s face. “We hadn’t been there long,” she said. “Now you are making me sad. I’m going to sleep. We will need our energy tomorrow when we reach the refinery.” She pulled on her breathing mask, wrapped her small frame in a blanket, and lay on the floor with her back to Omak.

Omak sat for a long time, keeping the fire going and staring at Rosa’s back. Some doubt gnawed at him. Something wasn’t right but he couldn’t quite figure out what. In the end, he dozed on and off until early morning.

It was midday by the time they reached the refinery. As they drew nearer, the sand turned grey and a thin mist filled the air. The refinery stood on a flat plain next to a dried river bed. It looked like a giant toddler had found a mountain of rusting scrap metal and poured sand all over it. Brown rusty towers poked out through the grit and sand that buried everything. A cave entrance gaped at the front of this huge pile like a toothless mouth.

"She's in there," Rosa said pointing to the cave.

Omak noticed Silva's and Turgen's buggies half buried in the sand. "The two buggies together," Omak muttered. "I thought you said there was no sign of Turgen..."

Omak didn't get to finish his sentence. Stars flared before his eyes and pain blistered through the back of his head as something heavy hit him and then all went dark.

CHAPTER 5

Gradually, Omak woke up. His head thumped and the room spun around him. Silva's face swam into focus. Her face was smudged with dirt and she had a cut on her forehead but she looked unharmed.

"Omak!" she said, shaking him. "Are you OK? What are you doing here?"

"I came to find you," he groaned. "Something hit me in the back of the head. Rosa…"

"You mean her?" Silva said, nodding towards the door.

They were lying in a dark cell with metal walls. Rosa's eyes glinted through the barred window in the thick door. He could see the wicked smile that stretched her face. He noticed her sharp teeth more now. She looked less human. "You're awake, then," she hissed at him.

"What are you up to?" Omak shouted. "Why did you bring me here?"

Rosa gave a horrible giggle. "Oh, you'll find out soon enough," she said. "Just like the other boy did…"

Silva leaped forward and tried to ram her fingers through the bars into Rosa's eyes but Rosa was too fast. With a hiss she pulled away and vanished into the shadows behind the door. Silva fell sobbing to the floor.

"I'm sorry, Omak, you were right," she said. "It was a foolish mission. There's nothing here but death."

Omak sat next to Silva in the straw. "What happened?"

"We arrived here quickly," Silva said, scrubbing the tears from her eyes. "Turgen wanted to go straight in and start exploring but I said we should wait and check around the outside first to see if it was safe. He didn't listen and charged in. Then they were all over us."

"They?" Omak felt his neck prickle. "Who?"

Silva shrugged. "People… creatures… I don't know what they are," she said. "They look human but smaller. Some of them are covered in sores and boils. Their teeth are sharp. They must be some kind of mutant race. There are thousands of them down here."

"Trogs," Omak muttered.

"What?" Silva said, frowning at him.

"The old man said something before he died," Omak said. "He told me to beware of the trogs.

I didn't know what he meant then. I think I do now."

Silva pulled a face. "Trogs," she repeated. "Comes from the word troglodyte. It means a cave-dweller."

"How could I have been so stupid not to think that something would be down here?" Omak snapped, jumping to his feet. He kicked at the door and stumbled back.

"Omak, stop," Silva said. "If we'd listened to you, we wouldn't be here. If it's anyone's fault, it's mine."

"Where is Turgen?" Omak said.

"I don't know." Silva looked pale in the half-light of the prison. "They took him away when we first got here and that's the last time I saw him."

Omak put a hand on Silva's shoulder. "Don't worry," he said. "If he's still alive, we'll find him." He turned his attention to the door. "Do we have anything we could use to loosen the rivets on the hinges?" he said, patting his pockets.

Silva turned out the pockets of her dusty overalls to reveal a few nuts and bolts. "I was saving this for a last fight," she whispered and revealed an emergency flare tucked down her sock.

"Amazing," Omak muttered. "How did you manage to hang onto that?"

"They don't seem very bright," she replied. "At least, not the ones that captured us. They took our backpacks but didn't search us."

At that moment, the door rattled open and what seemed like an army of mutants burst into the room. Omak and Silva were slammed to the floor and sharp spears were pointed into their faces.

Omak could see the mutants clearly now. They were small and pale like Rosa but many of them were stooped and covered in blisters and boils. They wore ragged trousers and the ripped remains of jackets but seemed to go barefoot.

Their eyes were big and almost colourless and their wide mouths brimmed with shark-like teeth. "You come with us," said one of the trogs, jabbing at Omak with his spear.

Omak and Silva were pushed and prodded down miles of twisting tunnels. "Look at the walls," Silva gasped. Pipes and torn cables snaked around each other along the sides of the passage and oil glistened, oozing and dripping over all of it. But growing through the oil was a web of fungus that glowed blue, illuminating their way.

Omak coughed. "The air is foul too. I can taste it," he spat.

They journeyed onward, going deeper. The air thickened and the ground beneath their feet grew sticky.

"This place must be covered in oil and petrol," Silva murmured.

Omak was about to reply but the sight before them shut him up. The blue fungus lit up a huge hall. It rose high above their heads and below them, a massive black lake filled the centre. In the middle of the lake, on a small island, sat a giant mutant. He was pale-skinned like the rest of the trogs who crowded around the banks of the lake. Boils and sores covered his skin. He held a long staff that had four human skulls stuck through the end of it like a kebab. He grinned and Omak swallowed hard. He'd never seen so many sharp, crooked teeth in one mouth.

"Down," the trog guard ordered, pointing at a rickety metal staircase that led down into the hall.

Omak glanced at Silva and started to clamber down the steps. Drumming filled the air and the trogs around the shores of the oil lake began to bow, moaning and shouting their praise to their giant ruler in the middle of the lake. The drums pounded faster as Silva and Omak approached the lake edge. The air stank of oil and the foul breath of the trogs who pressed in on them so that the guards had to beat them back with their spears.

"Look, a raft," Silva said.

"I think we're being taken to see the big boss himself," Omak replied as he was pushed onto the raft.

As they stepped onto the island, Omak's mouth went dry. The leader of the trogs looked even bigger when Omak got closer to him. Muscles rippled under his infected skin and two huge fangs poked up from his bottom jaw. He grinned at them and a black tongue slithered around his lips.

"Omak, look at the floor," Silva whispered.

Skulls and rib cages littered the slimy ground on which they stood. A huge axe was buried in a wooden block at the King Trog's feet.

"I think this is a slaughter house," Silva said faintly. "And I think we're next for the chopping block."

CHAPTER 6

The King Trog rose from his throne. "Welcome to my kingdom," the King Trog said. "I am Garn, Lord of the Trog people. You have come at a most important time."

"What do you want with us?" Omak snapped.

Garn gave a hideous chuckle. "I think you've already worked that out," he said. "My people hunger. They feed off rats and mice. They become restless whilst I plan but soon they will feast as richly as I do…"

"You monster," Silva yelled and threw herself forward. Garn swatted her away with one giant hand. Silva fell to the floor, dazed.

"We have been trapping unwary travellers for many years," Garn continued. "Every now and then we let one go. They usually send back more. The old man you met for instance."

"It was a trick," Omak gasped.

"For every scrawny fool like him we throw back into the desert, two fresher specimens come to us. The promise of rich oil and petrol reserves brings many foolhardy youngsters," Garn said. "They are easily overwhelmed by my people. But with so many mouths to feed, such tricks aren't enough!"

Omak shuddered. *I have to keep him talking,* he thought. *So I can figure out a way for us to escape.* "What do you mean?"

"My people grow in numbers, they hunger, they want more meat," Garn continued. "I tortured the location of the city out of the boy so that Rosa could go and examine its defences before she gave herself up to your Mayor."

"You monster!" Omak shivered. He tried not to think of poor Turgen. "Rosa was spying on us?" Out of the corner of his eye he noticed Silva slowly coming round.

"Soon, my people will swarm into the sewers under your city," Garn said. "We outnumber the people of the city. We will lose many but the feasting shall be great when the battle is won."

"No!" Omak shouted but Garn just laughed and wrapped his enormous fist around the handle of the axe.

"You and the girl are honoured," Garn said. "Rosa brought you to be our War Feast along with the girl. A small taste of the tender meat that awaits all of my people in the city. Because tomorrow, we attack!"

Omak gasped as Garn's fingers closed around his throat. The blue light glinted on the axe blade as Garn raised it high.

This is it, Omak thought, *I'm dead.*

Garn's fingers tightened and Omak's vision blurred. Then the dim blue light exploded into brilliant red. Fire filled the world and Omak fell to the ground, able to breathe again. He blinked and saw Silva holding the emergency flare. Garn had let go of him and was charging towards her now.

Silva thrust the flare forward into Garn's chest and the giant mutant burst into flame. Years of living underground amongst the oil had made his body super-flammable. Flames flickered across his chest and shoulders, and crackled through his wiry hair. He fell to the floor, beating at himself, trying to kill the fire that was consuming his body.

Silva didn't wait, though, she grabbed Omak's arm and dragged him onto the raft. Still dazed, he watched as she paddled them away.

"Silva, look!" he croaked. Ahead of them the crowd of trogs on the shore of the lake gathered, shaking spears angrily and snarling at them. "We're trapped!"

At that moment, the blazing Garn gave one last angry yell and charged after them, over the edge of the island and into the lake. Silence fell over the whole cavern for a split second as the trogs watched their leader vanish into the black oily lake. Then screams filled the air as the lake caught fire and exploded.

Omak and Silva's raft flew through the air and they landed, crushing five fleeing trogs. Flames spread everywhere now. The trogs were no longer interested in Omak or Silva. Everyone in that cavern just wanted to get out.

Omak and Silva grabbed a spear each and swung them around, clearing a space, knocking trogs out of their path. Choking black smoke filled the chamber, making it hard to see or breathe. They hurried up the metal stairs. The heat grew as the flames got larger and spread around the walls, fed by the oil that dripped down them.

"The tunnels will become like an oven if we don't hurry!" Silva yelled, coughing and spluttering.

It grew hotter and hotter. Trogs fell under Omak and Silva's feet, some leaped over their heads and the smoke grew thicker.

Silva stumbled and Omak grabbed her hand. "Look, daylight! We're near the exit!" He panted.

Something smashed into his side, sending him sprawling and small fingers wrapped around his throat. He looked up into the mad, staring eyes of Rosa. "You ruined everything!" she spat, banging his head to the ground. "Everything!" She opened her mouth wide to reveal needle-sharp teeth. Saliva drooled down her chin. "I'll rip your throat out for this!"

Omak wriggled and kicked but she had pinned him tight to the ground. He couldn't believe her strength. Then Silva appeared behind her and dragged her back. Rosa turned and lashed sharp nails across Silva's cheek, just missing her eyes. Silva swung her fist down and sent Rosa stumbling back into the dense smoke.

A loud rumble shook the whole tunnel and the earth jumped beneath their feet.

"Run!" Omak yelled. "The whole place is going to blow!"

Hand in hand, Omak and Silva hurried outside into the hot daylight. A muffled boom behind them sent them sprinting across the sand towards their buggies. The world became a storm of sand and flame. A roar like some kind of ancient beast deafened Omak. Rocks and metal flew everywhere, bouncing off the earth, whistling through the air.

The force of the blast threw Omak to the ground. He covered the back of his head with his hands, praying nothing heavy would hit him.

And then all fell silent, apart from the echo of the explosion drifting across the desert and the sound of metal and rock thumping and clinking to the ground.

Groaning, Omak dragged himself to his feet. "Silva?" he called. A fog of dust and smoke filled the desert. A shape came out of the mist. It was Rosa, soaked in blood, face twisted into a snarl. She held a metal bar and staggered towards Omak.

Omak's head spun. The air was poisoned. He'd been beaten and battered in the explosion. He blinked, trying to stay conscious. Rosa raised the metal club. She swayed a little, blinking at Omak, then collapsed on the ground.

Omak ran over to the Blood Bug and cleared the dirt that had half buried it. He pulled his breathing mask from inside and also grabbed one for Silva. He searched round, finding bodies of trogs caught nearer to the blast. At last he found Silva, dragging herself out of a huge pile of sand.

"We made it, Omak!" she gasped. "We made it."

The dust slowly settled to reveal a huge pit where the refinery had been. Flames still flicked at its bottom and twisted iron dotted its sides. There were no trogs to be seen anywhere.

They dug their cars free from the earth that had been thrown on top of them and hitched up Turgen's buggy to the back of the Blood Bug.

"Come on," Omak said. "Let's go home."

AFTER

Omak and Silva stood in the Council Chamber, smiling at the applause from the people around the room. Omak could see his mum beaming with pride as he received the Citizen Medal for special service to the city.

"The Award isn't just a medal," the Mayor announced. "It comes with extra food and water rations for the rest of your life, Omak."

Omak smiled. "Thank you, it's a great honour," he said. "But could those rations be directed to my mum?"

The Mayor nodded. "Of course! So, Omak, are you keen to get back into the driving seat again?"

Omak looked at Silva and then over at his mum and Fergal. "I might drive out every now and then, but I can't think of a more honourable job than working on the city water works."

Silva grinned. "What's up, Omak? Lost your taste for adventure?"

Omak shook his head. "You wish," he said, grinning.

THE END

ABOUT THE AUTHOR

Jon Mayhew lives near Liverpool with his family. He has written numerous books, including the award-winning *Mortlock* horror trilogy and the *Monster Odyssey* series. His other title for Teen Reads is *Death Road* which is set in the same world and has the same characters as this book.